P9-DJL-548

Sylvester
and the
MAGIC PEBBLE

by William Steig

Simon & Schuster Books for Young Readers
NEW YORK   LONDON   TORONTO   SYDNEY

To Maggie, Lucy, and Jemmy

SIMON & SCHUSTER BOOKS FOR YOUNG READERS ∼ An imprint of Simon & Schuster
Children's Publishing Division, 1230 Avenue of the Americas, New York, New York 10020 ∼
Copyright © 1969 by William Steig ∼ Copyright renewed © 1997 by William Steig ∼ All rights
reserved, including the right of reproduction in whole or in part in any form. ∼ SIMON &
SCHUSTER BOOKS FOR YOUNG READERS is a trademark of Simon & Schuster, Inc. ∼ Book design
by Dan Potash ∼ The text for this book is set in Golden Cockerel. ∼ The illustrations for this
book are rendered in watercolor. ∼ Manufactured in China ∼ 1120 SCP

18 20 19 17

Library of Congress Cataloging-in-Publication Data ∼ Steig, William, 1907–2003 ∼ Sylvester
and the magic pebble / William Steig.— 1st ed. ∼ p. cm. ∼ Caldecott Medal, 1970 ∼ Summary:
In a moment of fright, Sylvester the donkey asks his magic pebble to turn him into a rock but
then cannot hold the pebble to wish himself back to normal again. ∼ ISBN-13: 978-1-4169-0206-5
ISBN-10: 1-4169-0206-6 ∼ [1. Donkeys—Fiction. 2. Magic—Fiction. 3. Missing children—
Fiction.] I. Title. ∼ PZ7.S8177Sy 2005 ∼ [Fic]—dc22 ∼ 2004015445

Sylvester Duncan lived with his mother and father at Acorn Road in Oatsdale. One of his hobbies was collecting pebbles of unusual shape and color.

On a rainy Saturday during vacation he found a quite extraordinary one. It was flaming red, shiny, and perfectly round, like a marble. As he was studying this remarkable pebble, he began to shiver, probably from excitement, and the rain felt cold on his back. "I wish it would stop raining," he said.

To his great surprise the rain stopped. It didn't stop gradually as rains usually do. It CEASED. The drops vanished on the way down, the clouds disappeared, everything was dry, and the sun was shining as if rain had never existed.

In all his young life Sylvester had never had a wish gratified so quickly. It struck him that magic must be at work, and he guessed that the magic must be in the remarkable-looking red pebble. (Where indeed it was.) To make a test, he put the pebble on the ground and said, "I wish it would rain again." Nothing happened. But when he said the same thing holding the pebble in his hoof, the sky turned black, there was lightning and a clap of thunder, and the rain came shooting down.

"What a lucky day this is!" thought Sylvester. "From now on I can have anything I want. My father and mother can have anything they want. My relatives, my friends, and anybody at all can have everything anybody wants!"

He wished the sunshine back in the sky, and he wished a wart on his left hind fetlock would disappear, and it did, and he started home, eager to amaze his father and mother with his magic pebble. He could hardly wait to see their faces. Maybe they wouldn't even believe him at first.

As he was crossing Strawberry Hill, thinking of some of the many, many things he could wish for, he was startled to see a mean, hungry lion looking right at him from behind some tall grass. He was frightened. If he hadn't been so frightened, he could have made the lion disappear, or he could have wished himself safe at home with his father and mother.

He could have wished the lion would turn into a butterfly or a daisy or a gnat. He could have wished many things, but he panicked and couldn't think carefully.

"I wish I were a rock," he said, and he became a rock.

The lion came bounding over, sniffed the rock a hundred times, walked around and around it, and went away confused, perplexed, puzzled, and bewildered. "I saw that little donkey as clear as day. Maybe I'm going crazy," he muttered.

And there was Sylvester, a rock on Strawberry Hill, with the magic pebble lying right beside him on the ground, and he was unable to pick it up. "Oh, how I wish I were myself again," he thought, but nothing happened. He had to be touching the pebble to make the magic work, but there was nothing he could do about it.

His thoughts began to race like mad. He was scared and worried. Being helpless, he felt hopeless. He imagined all the possibilities, and

eventually he realized that his only chance of becoming himself again was for someone to find the red pebble and to wish that the rock next to it would be a donkey. Someone would surely find the red pebble—it was so bright and shiny—but what on earth would make them wish that a rock were a donkey? The chance was one in a billion at best.

Sylvester fell asleep. What else could he do? Night came with many stars.

Meanwhile, back at home, Mr. and Mrs. Duncan paced the floor, frantic with worry. Sylvester had never come home later than dinner time. Where could he be? They stayed up all night wondering what had happened, expecting that Sylvester would surely turn up by morning. But he didn't, of course. Mrs. Duncan cried a lot and Mr. Duncan did his best to soothe her. Both longed to have their dear son with them.

"I will never scold Sylvester again as long as I live," said Mrs. Duncan, "no matter what he does."

At dawn, they went about inquiring of all the neighbors.

They talked to all the children—the puppies, the kittens, the colts, the piglets. No one had seen Sylvester since the day before yesterday.

They went to the police. The police could not find their child.

All the dogs in Oatsdale went searching for him. They sniffed behind every rock and tree and blade of grass, into every nook and gully of the

neighborhood and beyond, but found not a scent of him. They sniffed the
rock on Strawberry Hill, but it smelled like a rock. It didn't smell like Sylvester.

After a month of searching the same places over and over again, and inquiring of the same animals over and over again, Mr. and Mrs. Duncan no longer knew what to do. They concluded that something dreadful must have happened, and that they would probably never see their son again. (Though all the time he was less than a mile away.)

They tried their best to be happy, to go about their usual ways. But their usual ways included Sylvester and they were always reminded of him. They were miserable. Life had no meaning for them any more.

Night followed day and day followed night over and over again. Sylvester on the hill woke up less and less often. When he was awake, he was only hopeless and unhappy.

He felt he would be a rock forever and he tried to get used to it. He went into an endless sleep. The days grew colder. Fall came with the leaves changing color. Then the leaves fell and the grass bent to the ground.

Then it was winter. The winds blew, this way and that. It snowed. Mostly, the animals stayed indoors, living on the food they had stored up.

One day a wolf sat on the rock that was Sylvester and howled and howled because he was hungry.

Then the snows melted. The earth warmed up in the spring sun and things budded. Leaves were on the trees again. Flowers showed their young faces.

One day in May, Mr. Duncan insisted that his wife go with him on a picnic. "Let's cheer up," he said. "Let us try to live again and be happy even though Sylvester, our angel, is no longer with us." They went to Strawberry Hill.

Mrs. Duncan sat down on the rock. The warmth of his own mother sitting on him woke Sylvester up from his deep winter sleep. How he wanted to shout, "Mother! Father! It's me, Sylvester, I'm right here!" But he couldn't talk. He had no voice. He was stone-dumb.

Mr. Duncan walked aimlessly about while Mrs. Duncan set out the picnic food on the rock—alfalfa sandwiches, pickled oats, sassafras salad, timothy compote. Suddenly Mr. Duncan saw the red pebble. "What a fantastic pebble!" he exclaimed. "Sylvester would have loved it for his collection." He put the pebble on the rock.

They sat down to eat. Sylvester was now as wide awake as a donkey that was a rock could possibly be. Mrs. Duncan felt some mysterious excitement. "You know, Father," she said suddenly, "I have the strangest feeling that our dear Sylvester is still alive and not far away."

"I am, I am!" Sylvester wanted to shout, but he couldn't. If only he had realized that the pebble resting on his back was the magic pebble!

"Oh, how I wish he were here with us on this lovely May day," said Mrs. Duncan. Mr. Duncan looked sadly at the ground. "Don't you wish it too, Father?" she said. He looked at her as if to say, "How can you ask such a question?"

Mr. and Mrs. Duncan looked at each other with great sorrow.

"I wish I were myself again, I wish I were my real self again!" thought Sylvester.

And in less than an instant, he was!

You can imagine the scene that followed—the embraces, the kisses, the questions, the answers, the loving looks, and the fond exclamations!

When they had eventually calmed down a bit, and had gotten home, Mr. Duncan put the magic pebble in an iron safe. Some day they might want to use it, but really, for now, what more could they wish for? They all had all that they wanted.

The End

William Steig's Caldecott Award Acceptance[*]

The last time I spoke formally to a group of people anywhere near this size was over a half-century ago, at P.S. 53 in the Bronx. I very quickly got tongue-tied and forgot what I was supposed to say. I have avoided this kind of confrontation ever since then. I was a poor speaker at age ten, and I've grown rustier with the years. So—to reduce my discomfort, and yours—I shall make this a short speech. Anyway, as a matter of form, it should not be as long as the little book that landed me here.

Among the things that affected me most profoundly as a child—and consequently as an adult—were certain works of art: Grimm's fairy tales, Charlie Chaplin movies, Humperdinck's opera *Hansel and Gretel*, the Katzenjammer Kids, *Pinocchio. Pinocchio* especially. I can still remember after this long stretch of time the turmoil of emotions, the excitement, the fears, the delights, and the wonder with which I followed Pinocchio's adventures.

William Steig signing a copy of *Sylvester and the Magic Pebble*

Often, at work or in everyday living, I do things or have experiences for which I find symbols that somehow derive from Collodi's great book. Recently I had a dream in which I was being led towards a place of judgment by two policemen, each with a firm grip on one of my arms. No doubt I was feeling guilty about something. But the scene was right out of a similar episode in *Pinocchio*, and I am sure that was its derivation. And it is very likely that Sylvester became a rock and then again a live donkey because I had once been so deeply impressed with Pinocchio's longing to have his spirit encased in flesh instead of in wood.

I am well aware not only of the importance of children—whom we naturally cherish and who also embody our hopes for the future—but also of the importance of what we provide for them in the way of art; and I realize that we are competing with a lot of other cultural influences, some of which beguile them in false directions.

Art, including juvenile literature, has the power to make any spot on earth the living center of the universe; and unlike science, which often gives us the illusion of understanding things we really do not understand, it helps us to know life in a way that still keeps before us the mystery of things. It enhances the sense of wonder. And wonder is respect for life. Art also stimulates the adventurousness and the playfulness that keep us moving in a lively way and that lead to useful discovery.

Books for children are something I take very seriously. I am hopeful that more and more the work I do for children, as well as the work I do for adults, will approach the condition of art. I believe that what this award and this ceremony represent is our mutual striving in the same direction, and I feel encouraged by the faith you have expressed in me in honoring my book with the Caldecott Medal.

I want to express my appreciation and gratitude to my friend and publisher, Bob Kraus of Windmill Books, who had the insight that I—and others like me—could make a contribution in this field, and who, because he himself is an artist, recognizes that the artist-publisher relationship is a symbiotic relationship, mutually beneficial not only in terms of monetary reward but in the more lasting reward of producing worthwhile work and being culturally useful.

Finally, I want to say that I still feel the pleasure and the gratitude that I felt when Mary Elizabeth Ledlie telephoned me from Chicago. And I love you all. I love you because you must love me. Anyway, that's how I understand your liking my work, which is a large part of me. Thank you.

---

* Given at the meeting of the American Library Association in Detroit, Michigan, on June 30, 1970. The Caldecott Medal for "the most distinguished American picture book for children" was awarded to William Steig for *Sylvester and the Magic Pebble* (Windmill Simon).